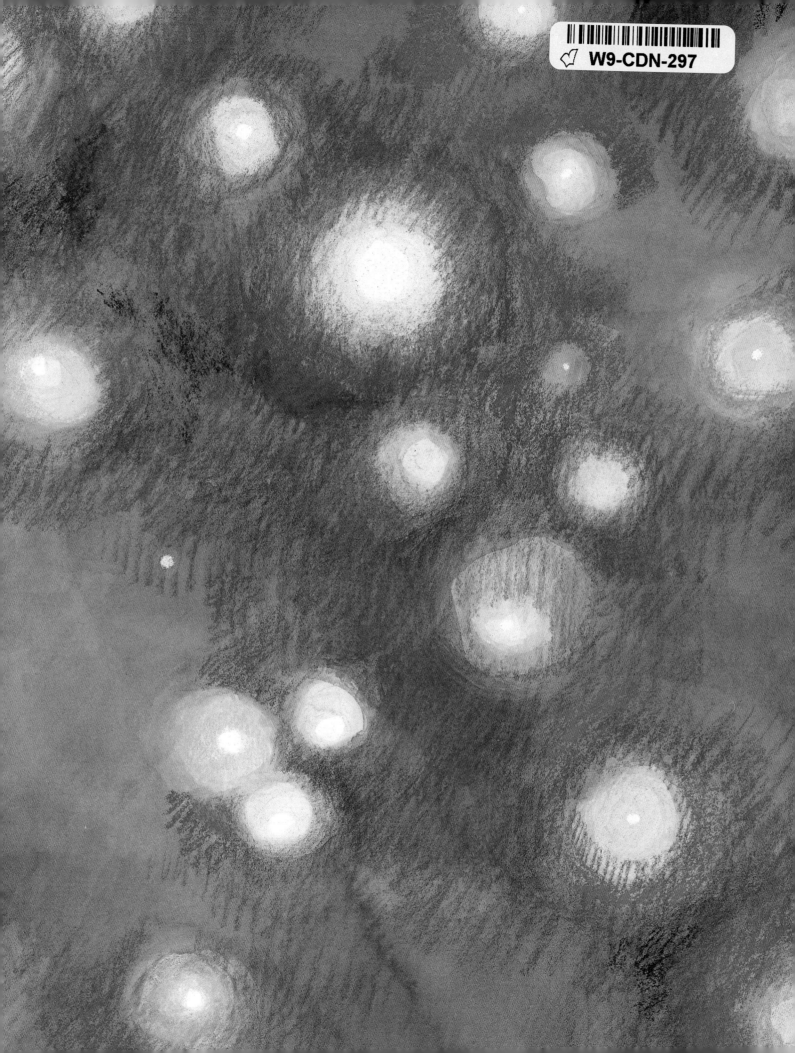

the
TINY STAR

For Elaine, with a twinkle —M.F.

For Helen, shining brightly —F.B.

THIS IS A BORZOI BOOK PUBLISHED BY ALFRED A. KNOPF

Text copyright © 2019 by Mem Fox
Jacket art and interior illustrations copyright © 2019 by Freya Blackwood

Visit us on the Web! rhcbooks.com

Educators and librarians, for a variety of teaching tools, visit us at RHTeachersLibrarians.com

Library of Congress Cataloging-in-Publication Data
Names: Fox, Mem, author. | Blackwood, Freya, illustrator.
Title: The tiny star / Mem Fox ; [illustrated by] Freya Blackwood.
Description: First American edition. | New York : Alfred A. Knopf, 2021. | "Originally published by Puffin Books, an imprint of Penguin Random House Australia Pty Ltd, Australia, in 2019"—Copyright page. | Audience: Ages 4–8. | Summary: "A star falls to earth where it becomes a baby and is embraced and cared for by the community."—Provided by publisher.
Identifiers: LCCN 2020050939 (print) | LCCN 2020050940 (ebook) | ISBN 978-0-593-30401-3 (hardcover) | ISBN 978-0-593-30402-0 (library binding) | ISBN 978-0-593-30403-7 (ebook)
Subjects: CYAC: Stars—Fiction.
Classification: LCC PZ7.F8373 Ti 2021 (print) | LCC PZ7.F8373 (ebook) | DDC [E]—dc23

The text of this book is set in 13-point Antihistory Regular.
Book design by Marina Messiha

MANUFACTURED IN CHINA
October 2021
10 9 8 7 6 5 4 3 2 1

First American Edition

the TINY STAR

MEM FOX & FREYA BLACKWOOD

ALFRED A. KNOPF
NEW YORK

Once upon a time, although this happens all the time, a tiny star fell to earth and turned into a baby!

The people who found it loved it immediately.

They took it home carefully

and wrapped it warmly

in a quilt all covered in stars.

Everyone agreed it was the most beautiful baby
they had ever seen.

The baby grew rounder

and rounder,

and taller and taller.

And even taller than that,
until one day

it was all grown up.

It was caring and kind,
and loving and wise,
and was loved and adored in return.

It had family and friends,
and hopes and dreams,

and a life that it lived to the full.

It grew older and older,
and older still.
And even older than that.

The longer it lived, the more it was loved.

Its family and friends
took great care of it.

They treated it gently
and wrapped it warmly
in a quilt all covered in stars.

The years passed.
It grew smaller and smaller,
and smaller still.

And even smaller than that,

until it was tiny once again . . .

so tiny it disappeared
altogether.

No one could believe it.
They ran to each other
and clung to each other
to comfort each other
and cry with each other.

But the tiny star hadn't vanished at all!
It had merely returned to its home in the heavens,
and there it remained, to rest.

What a sensation it was when it was seen again,
twinkling in the night sky.

Every heart was lightened.
Every heart began to mend.

From that time onward, everyone knew
that the star they had loved so much
would be there always,
loving them from afar and watching over them . . .

forever.

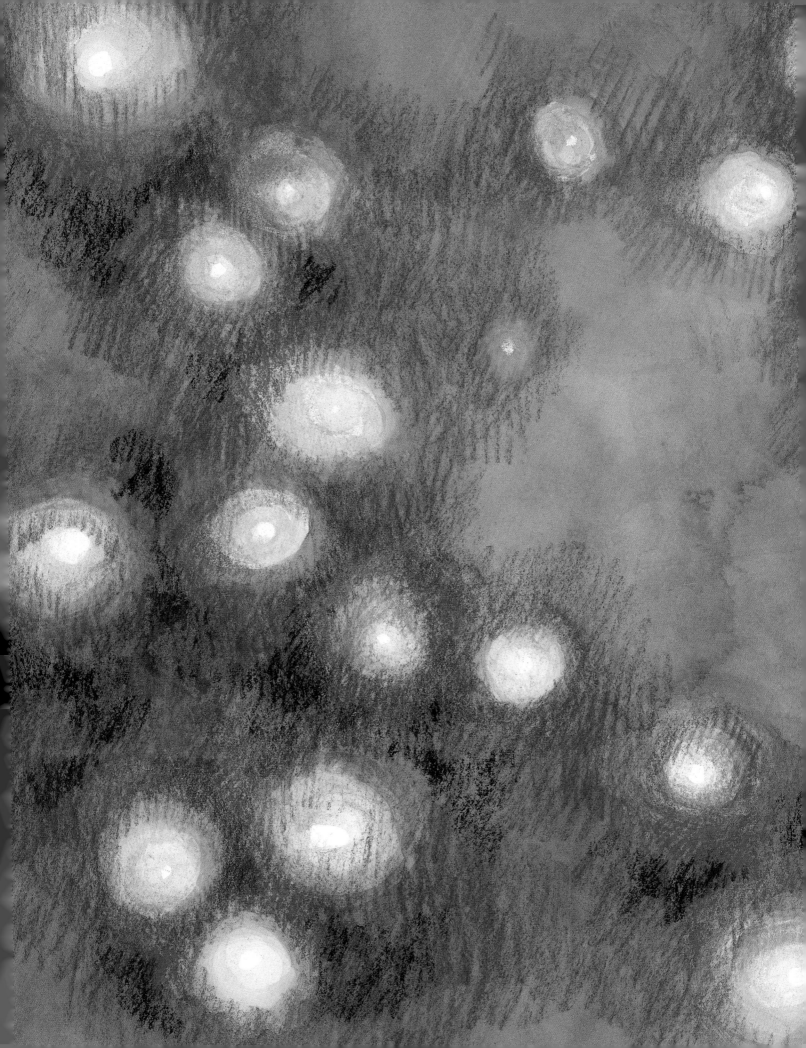